Torn

A TATTERED HEART DUET #1

USA TODAY BESTSELLING AUTHOR

BROOKE O'BRIEN

TORN

Ryan Blake is off limits. She is everything I shouldn't want, but do.

She's my best friend's sister, so feelings for her are out of the question. Her passion and fire trigger a spark in the dark hollows of my heart.

Now she's turning eighteen, and my resolve is starting to wear thin. I know I don't deserve her, but I can't walk away.

No matter how my heart aches for her, I know I'll tear her heart in two.

Thank you for reading **TORN**, the first book in the Tattered Heart Duet.

You can join my Facebook group, Brooke O'Brien's Rebel Reader Group, to discuss the series and get sneak peeks on future releases. Sign up for my newsletter to find out more about my

new releases. To join, visit: www.authorbrook
eobrien.com/follow.

Enjoy Mav & Ryan's story!

Tattered Heart Duet
READING ORDER

TORN

TATTERED

a brother's best friend, military romance

Learn more and purchase your copy at:
www.authorbrookeobrien.com/tatteredheart
duet

DEDICATION

This book is dedicated to anyone struggling to find their worth and to the brave souls who love them enough to stick around to help them see it.

Prologue

MAVERICK

It was never my intention to fall in love with my best friend's sister. I was thirteen when I moved down the street from Dean Blake. He had come into my life at a time I struggled to cope with the world around me. Our friendship came without any pressures, it was easy. He didn't ask questions, but I think he knew what would happen if he did.

I closed off the door to my heart a long time ago. I didn't want to feel. The pain that comes with letting the emotions in is more than I could ever bear. Even through it all, I still remember the way I felt when I met his twin sister, Ryan.

It was like a jolt to my heart, forcing it to beat out of rhythm.

Ryan was all legs, chocolate brown hair flowing in the breeze covered by her backward snapback. The first thing I noticed was the intricate detail of the designs covering her skin, like vines wrapping around her arm.

If the sweet and innocent look on her face was any indication, she was too young to have tattoos of her own. I was drawn to the outward shell she presented to the world because I recognized it for what it was. A distraction from all the parts you want to keep buried deep. She was like a mirage of walking contradictions, which I knew to be true the moment she opened her smart mouth.

The passion she withheld under the surface was like a beacon of light shining in the dark night. Her fiery personality was the first thing to trigger a spark in the hollows of my heart.

All these years I've spent keeping my distance from her, out of fear of facing my feelings and the consequences that could follow. The hard part is, I know she feels the connection between us, too. The pull that keeps us tethered to each other, despite never allowing her to get close enough.

She's turning eighteen in two days and the resistance I've been struggling to keep hold of is starting to wear thin. Nothing good can come from going down this path because no matter how much my heart aches for her, it's inevitable I'll leave her heart torn in two.

Chapter One

RYAN

"Roll the window down, it smells like sex in here!" I shout, waving my hand in front of my face. Sticking my head outside, I take a deep breath and turn my head toward my best friend with a shit eating grin on my face.

"Says the virgin," she mutters, rolling her eyes as she turns up the music to drown out any smart-ass reply I could fire back. I know she can hear me as I tell her to fuck off, which prompts her to wave her middle finger in the air at me while keeping her eyes on the road.

Papa Roach blares through the speakers, as I slide back into my seat adjusting my hat as I do. I can feel the energy from the music run through my body as I nod my head to the lyrics.

Nadia is my best friend, my A1 since day one. There's not much I wouldn't do for her and I knew it to be true from the day we first met.

We were in eighth grade, riding the bus to school, when Kara Parker thought it would be fucking funny to pick shit out of the garbage and throw it at me from where she sat in the back. She only messed with me on the days my twin brother, Dean, would opt to walk to school with his friends.

She knew better than to pull that shit around Dean.

Nadia had been sitting in the seat across from me. It was the first day we had ever talked to each other. After watching a pop bottle cap whiz past our heads, she turned toward me with her face hard as stone as she said, "You ready to put this bitch down?"

My response mirrored the same devilish grin she flashed me. She's been my ride or die ever since.

"Did you talk to your mom about staying over at my place tomorrow?" she asks, shouting over the music. Nadia's parents take on the role of parenting from a distance. They leave her money on the counter and make sure there's always food in the cabinets. Otherwise, they're hardly home, which makes it the perfect place to crash when we plan to hit up a party or two on the weekends.

"She hasn't responded to my text message yet," I mutter, clicking the button on the side of my phone to check for a response. "I'm going to call her and see." Leaning over, I turn down the radio as I click the call button.

"Big Papa's Pizzeria."

My brother's immature greeting has me rolling my eyes so hard I'm surprised they didn't pop out of my head and roll across the floor. The worst part is the annoying laugh that follows finding his lame joke funny.

"Put Mom on the phone," I snap, cutting off his obnoxious laughter, running my fingers over the frayed hole in my jeans.

"What's in it for me?"

"Staying alive. Now quit being a prick, dick licker, and put her on the phone."

"You wanna talk to your mom with that dirty mouth?" Dean laughs. I can hear the light chuckling in the background, and if I had to guess, Maverick is there with him.

Figures.

"Seriously, D. I don't have all night. If I don't talk to her now, I'm going to be home late."

"You better hope that's not the case. After the last time, you know you're going to end up grounded. Happy Birthday to you."

I can picture his smug face as he sings the last part to me and I seriously want to junk punch him.

"Alright, Dad. Noted. Now put her on the fucking phone."

I can hear the light rustling on the other end before my mom's overly chipper voice filters through the phone.

"Yes, Ryan," she says with a sigh.

"Hi, Mom," I reply, my tone extra sweet which has Nadia laughing. "Is it cool if I crash at Nadia's this weekend?"

"Not tonight, Ryan," she replies curtly. "You can tomorrow since it's your birthday, but it's not necessary to stay over two nights in a row."

"Can I stay out a little later tonight then instead? It's a Friday night and we were going to meet up with some friends."

"You've been late once already this month, even after I extended your curfew. You have until ten o'clock to be home, Ryan. By the looks of it, that gives you seventeen minutes. I'll see you soon."

Nadia glances down at the clock as the line disconnects.

"Ry, we're not going to make it in time," she says, voicing my thoughts. I don't say anything because she's right. My house is at least twenty-five minutes away on a good day.

"Shit," I groan, running my hand over my face.

Nadia does her best to get me home in time, but when we hit a train on Rockford Drive, I know it's no use.

"Look on the bright side," Nadia says, peering over at me out of the corner of her eye. "If Dean is home, that likely means Maverick is crashing at your house tonight."

Maverick is one of my brother's best friends, which is both a blessing and a curse. He and Dean never go anywhere without the other. Dean is the annoying, obnoxious jock who likes to have all the attention on him. Maverick, on the other hand, is the complete opposite and sometimes I wonder what prompted their friendship.

Don't get me wrong, Dean's my twin brother, and he's a great guy. I don't know what they have in common besides skateboarding. Whatever it is, they are nearly inseparable. Maverick usually ends up staying over at our house, which I appreciate because it means I get to see him more.

"Like that matters. He acts as if I'm not there. I swear you'd think he hated me or something."

"I don't think that's true." Nadia laughs, shaking her head. "I think he's very much aware you're there. He just knows Dean would lose his shit if he knew he saw you as anything but his sister."

Which brings me to why it's a curse. Any chance of Maverick seeing me as more than his best friend's sister goes out the window. I know he would never do anything to put their friendship in jeopardy.

I can keep a secret and what Dean doesn't know won't hurt him.

Nadia whips the car into the driveway, pulling in behind Dean's beat-up Ford truck. The thing has seen better days, but he refuses to replace it.

"Text me when you can and let me know the damage," she mutters, clearly concerned our plans for tomorrow could be ruined.

I push the door of the car open and lean the seat forward, pulling out my skateboard from the backseat. I sling my backpack over my shoulder and readjust my hat on my head.

"Wish me luck," I groan, as I move the seat back in place.

We say our goodbyes as I head toward the front of my house.

My mom is in the kitchen loading the dishwasher when I enter the house. She doesn't bother to look at me, which I know can't be good. Kicking my shoes off near the door, I prop my board against the wall.

I spot Dean and Maverick lounging in the living room. Dean has his leg draped across the coffee table and a grin on his face, knowing what's about to come. Maverick grimaces and I know this can't be good.

"Welcome home," my mother says, the force of the dishwasher closing draws my attention away from him.

"Ryan, this is the second time you've been late this month. Before you even try to argue, I want to point out your birthday is in less than two hours, and I know you have plans with Nadia."

Dropping my bag down on the bench near the door, I slide the hat off my head and toss it on top before facing my mom.

"I'm sorry," I sigh, knowing nothing good will come from me saying anything more. "I'm going to bed."

I walk through the kitchen and into the living room. The urge to junk punch Dean has returned when I see the arrogant smirk on his face.

"Keep it up, fucker," I mutter under my breath, careful to not let my mom overhear us as I flash him the finger.

"What's that?" he retorts, turning his head to peer over the back of the couch.

Spinning around, I find both of their eyes on me. Seeing that my mom has since made her way out of the kitchen, likely retreating to our parents' bedroom, I don't hold back.

"I said keep it up, fucker. I should be the one laughin' at you, sitting at home like a bum on a Friday night," I snap, sounding bored as I lean against the wall.

There are about seven minutes separating the two of us. My parents were expecting to bring home two baby boys when I was born. What they didn't expect was for the second child to be born a girl. My name is evidence of that.

Dean turns around, facing the TV and lets out an annoyed grunt, "Fuck off, Ry."

My eyes bounce from Dean to Maverick and I'm surprised when I find Maverick's are already on me. They shine bright with amusement, as he bites his lower lip in an attempt to hide the grin lining his mouth. Crossing his arms over his chest, he runs his hand over his jaw as he glances over to make sure Dean isn't paying attention.

The thick muscles are tanned from all his days outside without his T-shirt on. His dark-brown hair is longer on top. The wayward strands give the appearance like he has ran his fingers through them one too many times.

The sleeves of my white T-shirt are cut off, giving it more of a muscle-shirt look. You can see my black sports bra from the side and a hint of my sun-kissed skin underneath.

My heart starts to pound as I relish the thought of him struggling to take his eyes off me. Taking two steps backward, I keep my eyes trained on him. I think back to my conversation with Nadia in the car when she said it's Dean that's holding him back.

The bold side of me wants to test her theory and see if it's true.

Standing outside my bedroom door, I keep my eyes focused on Maverick as I grab the hem of my shirt and pull the cotton material over my head. I roll my shirt into a ball before tossing it in the direction of my dirty clothes but not bothering to check if it made it.

I watch as Maverick's jaw clenches as his eyes travel over the length of my body, resting longer on my chest than necessary before finally bringing his eyes up to meet mine. He leans forward, pressing his elbows to his knees. Even then, he doesn't take his eyes off me.

"D, I'm gonna use your bathroom quick and head out. I should've been home a little while ago."

I can hear Dean mumble out a response, but I have no idea what he says. I'm too lost in the look on Maverick's face to pay much attention to what is going on around me.

Bracing his palms on his knees, Maverick moves to stand. He's so tall, standing over six feet. He's athletic, but whereas my brother is stockier from his time in football, Maverick is lean.

I can hear my heart pounding in my ears as he stalks toward me with a slight tic in his jaw. The closer he gets to me, the more my body comes alive with his presence.

"A little bold of you. Wouldn't you say, Rebel?"

It isn't the first time I've heard him use the nickname, but the tone in his voice is deeper. I can feel the words roll through me, crashing over me like waves as he stands close leaving only an inch between us.

I'm not able to think properly as I stare up at his gray eyes. They're so dark, it's almost like a storm is brewing in their depths.

Raising his hand up, he runs his knuckle along the soft skin of my shoulder as I force a step away from him. I need to gain some semblance of sanity, but the move causes his lip to curl in a small grin.

"You have nothing to say now? I didn't think that was possible." His quiet chuckle does crazy things to my heart.

"Aren't you supposed to be leaving now?" I retort, hating how he can look so unaffected knowing the way he's making me feel.

"Yeah, I am. Are you sure it's what you want though?"

He presses the palm of his hand against my hip as he moves to step closer in the narrow hallway. I'm standing so close to the wall, I know there's plenty of room for him to pass by.

His thumb lightly traces my exposed skin, as he takes a step around me. His body is pressed against mine, bringing us closer than we've ever been.

The move forces the air out of my chest and I know he can feel my body tremble beneath his touch.

"I didn't think so," he whispers against the shell of my ear.

As soon as he passes by me and the bathroom, he glances back at me. His eyes travel down to where my chest heaves with every struggled breath before looking back up at me. Flashing me a wink, he turns and walks down the hallway and out the front door without another word.

Holy shit.

Chapter Two

MAVERICK

Closing the front door behind me, I sag against it. Bracing my hands on my knees, I force a deep breath.

"Damn it," I mutter to myself.

Now I'm reminded why I've forced myself to stay away from her all these years. That glimpse of the way her body came alive under my touch sent my heart stuttering into a tailspin.

Once the adrenaline coursing through me slows, I grab my skateboard from where I left it leaning against the side of the stairs. Walking down the driveway and onto the sidewalk, I hold my board out in front of me. Jogging a few steps,

I plant my left foot as I use my other to pick up speed. The sound of the wheels rolling over every crack in the cement distracts me from my wayward thoughts.

I know I crossed a line with Ryan tonight. I'm not blind, I've noticed how she watches me. She tries to keep it subtle, not wanting to draw attention. Her gaze feels like fire, burning into me. I can only tell myself to ignore it for so long before I start to give in.

I've always found her unfiltered thoughts refreshing.

Hearing her smart mouth as she shot back at Dean had me unable to resist approaching her. The fire I saw in her gaze begged me to come closer. As soon as my hand touched the soft skin on her hip, it was going to be impossible for me to walk away.

If it weren't for the fact I knew what waited for me when I got home and knowing Dean was a few feet away, I would've never left.

The light from the lamppost at the end of the driveaway casts a soft glow on the wet cement as my skateboard takes me further away from Ryan. It doesn't take long before I'm turning the corner near my house. We're always the only house on the street without their front porch light on, making it difficult to see as I walk up the steps.

On the outside, you'd think no one was home, but I knew it wasn't true. What's waiting on the other side of the door is just as dark, but for a different reason. The thought alone makes me want to turn around and head back toward Dean and Ryan's house.

Pulling the keys from my pocket, I'm quiet as I stick the key in the lock and turn the door handle, pushing the door open. The house is quiet, other than the soft sound of the television playing. Slipping off my shoes, I tiptoe down the hall toward my bedroom. I'm careful to avoid the spots on the wooden floor that will creak with every step.

As soon as I turn the doorknob to my bedroom, I hear his husky voice bellow my name from the other room.

"Ryle." The word causes a chill to roll through my body. No one calls me by my middle name except for my father. You'd think he took pride in his son being named after him, but in fact it's the opposite. He calls me by his name out of spite. It's a reminder he's given me life and would take it away if I ever dared to challenge him.

I'm not the only person living in this house who has allowed the pain of the past to damage their heart.

Letting out a resigned sigh, I turn and make the two steps across the hall. The door is open a crack, so I raise my hand, pushing it open and stepping into the doorway.

"Yes?"

"Where the hell have you been all day? You were supposed to go up to the corner store and do the dishes. Neither of them got done."

"I'll do it in the morning when I wake up."

"What good is it going to do me now? I'm out of cigarettes," he grunts. I turned eighteen three weeks ago. Every day since I've made the trip up to the gas station to buy him smokes.

The light from the TV flashes, lighting his face. His beard is long, matching the greasy unkept hair on his head. If I had to guess, he's probably going on Day Seven since he's even bothered to clean himself up.

"It's after ten. They closed almost thirty minutes ago so there's not much I can do now. I'll make sure the dishes get done," I say, reaching down toward the door handle to pull it closed.

"You're an ungrateful piece of shit, you know that? Had you been home when you're supposed to, this wouldn't be a problem."

Forcing a deep inhale through my nose, I tighten my jaw resisting the urge to tell him to fuck off.

"I'll get to it then," I grit out, knowing he never cared when I came home before. Hell, he doesn't pay attention to me unless he needs me to do something or he's finding new ways to put me down.

"You know, you're eighteen now. I don't have to give you a roof over your fucking head anymore. I think it's time for you to get the hell outta my house." The anger is rising in his tone. When he yells, it exacerbates his emphysema, sending him into a coughing fit.

Knowing I'd be fighting a losing battle if I dared to respond, I back out of his bedroom and amble down the hall. My once quiet steps are now replaced with my rushed foot falls. I can hear his hoarse words behind me, but I do my best to push them out of my mind.

Shoving my feet into my sneakers, I pick up my skateboard from against the wall. Running my hands over my pockets, I double check to make sure I have my keys before I swing open the door and slip back into the dark night.

It isn't until I'm walking back up Dean's driveway that I'm able to breathe a calming sigh. Both lights on the front of the house are on so I know Dean and Ryan are still awake.

Sitting down on the front step, I run my hand over my face and pinch the bridge of my nose. I knew I shouldn't have been late going home. After I heard Dean on the phone with Ryan, I decided to sit back wanting a few minutes to see her.

It's been more and more difficult to go home lately. The anniversary of my mom's death looms, and as a result, my dad has been drinking more. His own health has begun to deteriorate.

My mom passed away when I was fifteen from breast cancer. My dad still carries a lot of guilt over it. He had lost his job about six months before, which meant my mom had started to pick up more hours at the local grocery store where she worked.

She was faithful about going to her annual checkups. Times were tough though, so when she was asked to pick up an extra shift she didn't hesitate in saying yes. There were nights I would lay up at night and hear them argue about money. The bills were starting to stock-pile, and we needed the extra money.

After she found a lump in her breast, she admitted to my dad she had missed rescheduling her appointment. He took it incredibly hard knowing she may have caught it then. She was at a stage four and the doctors felt chemo treatments would only give her another four to six months to live.

Chemo would've meant more days spent at the doctor's office or nights at the grocery store to pay for all the bills, when what she wanted to do was just enjoy what was left of her life.

To this day, I struggle with opening myself back up to anyone again out of fear of losing them unexpectedly. Dean and our friend, Graham, are the only two people I'm close to.

Thinking back to what happened between me and Ryan in the hall tonight fills me with a sense of guilt. I've heard the way guys at school talk about her. I have also listened to how Dean has reacted; his promises of violence if he heard those words repeated.

Ryan spent years hiding behind her baggy clothes and backward hats when she was younger. So, when she started wearing clothes that fit her, it left very little to the imagination.

She has been the star of many of my fantasies, more than I'd ever like to admit.

Maybe she wasn't interested or maybe it was Dean's persistent threats to anyone who came around Ryan, but she only had one boyfriend throughout high school. She would bring Marc around and I wanted to crawl out of my skin as I watched the subtle ways he'd touch her.

I remember one night when I left to head home, I saw Marc press her against the side of the house as he kissed her. Something about seeing his hands on her pissed me off. Instead of ignoring it and moving on, like I should've, I barreled toward them and told her to get her ass inside. I still cringe when I recall seeing them together, hating how much I sounded like Dean warning off anyone who dare look at her.

Pushing the memory out of my mind, I decide I've spent enough time sulking over my problems. At this point, I'm ready to lie down and try to get some sleep. I slide between the bushes lining the front of the house as I approach Dean's bedroom window. Reaching over, I lightly knock on the glass.

I stand here for a minute, waiting, before Dean pulls the blinds up enough for his head to peer out. As soon as his eyes adjust to the darkness, he holds up a finger signaling for me to give him a minute before he quickly closes the blinds again. I slip back through the bushes and climb the stairs toward the front door.

A few seconds later, Dean stands in the doorway as he runs his hands over his arms to keep them warm. The storms earlier tonight left the spring air cool. I've always loved this weather, so it doesn't bother me.

Dean doesn't say anything, not bothering to acknowledge how I had left less than an hour ago and here I am turning up at his door. He knows if I wanted to talk about it, I would. All I want to do is get some rest but as we pass by Ryan's door as we walk down the hall, all I can think about is how I wish I could be lying next to her right now.

Chapter Three

RYAN

The sound of footsteps in the hall jolt me awake. I've always been a light sleeper, waking up at even the faintest of sounds. Reaching my hand over toward my nightstand, I turn the alarm clock so the time is facing me. The red lights flash the time after midnight before I push it away.

Glancing around my room, my eyes adjust to the light. I had woken up an hour ago when I heard Dean let Maverick in. It happens often enough so I know when I hear the door open not to be too concerned.

Wondering if it could be him in the hallway, I can't stop myself from climbing out of bed to find out. Pulling a tank top out of my dresser, I run my hand through my hair to wrestle the long locks into submission as I quietly step out into the hallway.

I can hear the toilet flush followed by the sink turning on, as I lean against the wall waiting. The bathroom door swings open and the light flickers off, bathing us in darkness. I hear the subtle inhale of Maverick's breath and I wonder if it's because I've surprised him or from being alone with me once again.

"You waitin' for me or somethin'?" he grunts, trying to keep his voice down.

"No, I like to wait outside of bathrooms at twelve o'clock in the morning."

I can see his shoulders shake lightly as he covers up his laughter.

After our run in earlier tonight, of course I wanted to torment myself with more. I guess I'm just a glutton for punishment, but I've never been able to help myself where he's concerned.

"You going to move or do you want to join me?" I retort.

My eyes have adjusted to the darkness and I watch as he runs his hand over his jaw. I can make out the shadow from his arms and I want to reach my hand out to touch his sculpted skin. My eyes travel down his body to see him dressed in nothing but a pair of gym shorts.

"I'll move."

He steps out into the hallway, his body eating up the space as I find myself pressed against the wall once again. I relish the feel of the cold drywall against my heated skin.

Running my tongue along my bottom lip, I force a swallow trying to hide my heavy breathing. He leans in close to me, his breath feathering along the shell of my ear. I tilt my head back and clench my hands into fists, resisting the urge to pull his mouth to mine.

"You smell fuckin' amazing, Rebel. Like peaches and everything I shouldn't want."

His words rattle through my head as I lazily open my eyes. It's hard to see him in the darkness. Before I know it, he takes a step back to the other side of the hall and continues to run his hand over his jaw.

"Go before I do something we both may regret."

"What are you doing here? I thought you went home," I say, ignoring him.

"Change of plans," he says, folding his arms across his chest.

I can hear the edge in his tone, so I decide not to probe any further. Leaning against the wall, mimicking his pose.

"Where were you and Nadia tonight?"

"We went to the basketball game with some friends."

His eyes follow down my body to the boxer shorts I'm wearing as he nods his head.

"Basketball game, huh?"

I can hear the questioning in his tone. I've never been the type to watch sports. The extent of my physical activity has been riding dirt bikes or skateboarding.

"What are you trying to say?"

"You have never watched sports before. Hell, even when Dean tried to get you to come to one of his football games, it was like pulling teeth."

I narrow my eyes at him. "You don't strike me as somebody who knows a damn thing about me, Mav."

I'm not sure why I'm so defensive again at his statement. The condescending tone in his voice is grating my nerves raw.

I shoulder past him; I make it past the doorway of my bedroom when his warm hand wraps around my forearm stopping me. He doesn't hold onto me for long, as he presses his chest against my back, wrapping his arm around my waist.

I tilt my head against his shoulder when his mouth presses against the side of my head.

"I know a lot about you, Ryan Marie. More than you may think."

His words come out muffled and I can feel my body shiver.

Tracing his hand down my arm, he grasps my wrist and holds my arm out in front of me.

"I know you like to go skateboarding by yourself every Saturday and Sunday morning. Some mornings, when I'm sleeping over, I hear you wake up before anyone else to go. I know when you're having a bad day you like to blare *Disturbed*. I also know you never let a day go by where you're not drawing some sort of design on your skin. Despite what your mom might tell you, you want to fill your arm with the artwork you know will someday be permanently etched on your skin."

I don't know what to say because everything he said is the truth. I'm surprised to hear he's been watching me because, to my knowledge, he had never paid any attention. I always felt like he viewed me as the annoying sister of his best friend.

"I wish I knew what it meant to you," he whispers in my ear. "The words, the artwork. I know you well enough to know you wouldn't put something on your skin unless it meant something to you."

Looking down at his hand wrapped around my wrist, I watch as his thumb lightly traces back and forth over the heart on the inside of my wrist.

"I wish I knew why you knocked on Dean's bedroom window at all hours of the night. I guess there are a lot of things about ourselves we don't talk about with just anyone."

"You're right," he says as I tilt my head up to look him in the eye. "You're more than just anyone."

He lets go of my hand, letting it drop back against my side as he takes a step back. I should've expected this reaction. It's clearly something he doesn't want to talk about.

I'm taken by surprise when he doesn't move to leave, instead he eases his way around me, stepping further into my bedroom. The small lamp I turned on earlier adds a little light in the room and I'm distracted watching the way he moves confidently in the small space.

The muscles in his back move and I feel light-headed at the thought of running my hand over the smooth skin. If I was surprised before, I'm completely stunned when he dives onto my bed and rolls onto his side facing me.

My eyes run over his body, to the way the muscles of his abdomen tighten and the dark smattering of hair leading lower beneath his shorts. The sound of his throat clearing as my eyes wander back up until they meet his.

"What are you doing?"

"Oh, I thought we were going to exchange our stories, mine for yours. I wanted to get comfy." He winks as a small smile plays on the corner of his mouth.

I don't know what to do with this new side of Maverick.

"If that's the case, you'll need to move over unless you want me lying on top of you."

It was meant to come out as a joke, but I can see the thought cross Maverick's mind as he clears his throat.

I don't know how we've moved so quickly past the older brother's best friend zone to something entirely different, but I don't bother asking out of fear he'll realize we're treading on thin waters.

Taking two steps closer to him, I climb on the bed and lie down next to him. He moves over, making room for me.

"Tell me about the ink."

"I've always known after high school I wanted to pursue a career in art. I started drawing when I was in early elementary. It started off with coloring pencils but as I've grown older, it's moved into painting and oils. During school, I had a hard time focusing but drawing always helped me through it. The art on my arms all have symbolic meaning. They represent what I'm thinking and feeling."

Holding my arm out above us, I start going through all the handcrafted designs covering my forearm.

"Who is Evelyn?" he asks, glancing over at me before inspecting the name written on my wrist.

"It's my grandma on my dad's side. I got my passion for art from her. The roots," I say, pointing to the base of the vines wrapped around the side of my arm up toward my elbow, "remind me to stay grounded and the heart symbolizes focusing on where my heart lies."

"I like it," he says. "I've heard the way your mom talks about the designs on your arms, trying to convince you to wash them off. You never do though, at least not for long."

I can feel the smile play at my lips at the thought of him paying attention enough to notice it doesn't take long before I'm drawing something new.

"She certainly tries, but her efforts are futile. I think she's noticing, too. It's something I love. I'm not going to stop because she doesn't like it. I'm eighteen now and there's nothing she can do it about it," I say, realizing it's after midnight which means it's officially my birthday.

"Happy Birthday," he whispers. Reaching his hand out, he rubs the calloused skin of his thumb over my forearm.

My eyes follow the path before slowly traveling up to peer at him. When they connect with his, he drops my arm between us but doesn't move to let go.

"Thank you."

There is a closeness to him I've never felt, being alone together in the quietness of my bedroom. This is the most I've ever talked to Maverick. Normally, he's the quiet, shy guy who stands off to the side. He blends in well with

Dean and his friends. Most of them don't do much talking to begin with. I feel like there are so many questions on the edge of my tongue, waiting to be spoken.

"What do you think Dean would say if he woke up right now and found you in here with me?" I ask, flashing him a small smile.

We both know exactly how he would react. He's more than protective. He's like having a third parent, only more annoying if that's somehow possible.

"He'd probably threaten to kick my ass as he marched me out the door." He chuckles, releasing the hold he has around my arm as it sinks in how this could turn out if Dean did walk in on us lying together on my bed.

"Why? I mean, it's not like we're doing anything wrong. So, you're lying on my bed. Big deal. It's not like anything happened. We're talking."

His lip quirks up at the side, as if he finds my defensiveness amusing before moving his arms behind the back of his head. He rolls over onto his back, staring up at the stars glowing on the ceiling.

"I told you about my drawings. Those are personal for me. Now it's your turn. Tell me something no one else knows."

I don't know how much time passes as my eyes roam over the side of his face. The dark stubble on his cheeks adding a layer of definition to his perfectly sculpted face.

"I sneak out of my house every night to sneak into yours. Sometimes it's to outrun the nightmares of the life back home, other times it's to escape the demons that plague me in my dreams."

I wait for him to explain more, not wanting to push him. The deep sigh he releases feeling more like the weight of the boulder sitting heavily on his chest.

"It's my dad; he hasn't been the same since my mom passed away. When we found out she was diagnosed with cancer, we begged her to fight but it was too late. Stage four cancer doesn't leave you with a lot of hope, I guess. She wanted to enjoy what was left of her life.

"She struggled with the decision of whether to do chemo and I hated seeing how much the cancer was taking from her. I didn't want it to take the last few months we had with her. When I told her it was okay, my dad lost it.

He still blames me for it, for not convincing her to fight harder. I tell myself to just make it through the school year. I have enough credits to graduate early, but while I'm going to school, I can take extra college classes and they're paid for by the school. I want to take advantage of it while I can, ya know?"

Turning to lie on my side, I rest my cheek against my elbow listening to him. I want him to feel like I'm here with him, to know I care.

"It's okay though, really. He can be an asshole, but it's nothing I'm not used to. I try to steer clear of him when he's in his moods."

"I hate you have to sneak out to come over here."

"I like being here," he whispers. I can't help but wonder if he's talking about here, in my room. He adjusts his head, looking back up at the ceiling.

The time ticks by as my thoughts drift off, thinking about what life is like for him at home. My mind shuffles through the memories, pieces of information I've overheard and picked up over time.

Sliding into the backseat of my mom's old Volkswagen I reach back, grabbing the seat belt and click it into place. Glancing out the window, I listen as my mom and Dean bicker with each other about his choice in music.

A few minutes later, we pull into the driveway at Maverick's house. The grass is overgrown, and I notice one of the shutters is missing since the last time we were here. The sound of rain lightly beats down on the window.

The door swings open and Maverick steps out wearing a jacket. He has the hood pulled up, covering his face as he presses his chin against his chest. His body looks tense and I soon know the reason why, as his dad tears out the door, following him, causing the screen door to slam at the side of the house.

"What's going on?" my mom mutters quietly, voicing my thoughts out loud. "He asked permission if he could come with us, right?"

My eyes stay focused on Maverick. I watch as he grimaces. I can see the spit flying out of his dad's mouth as his finger points at him, shouting. Maverick nods his head, acknowledging him before turning back toward us, looking embarrassed and dejected.

"No, he just doesn't like him," Dean replies.

I wish I knew what his dad was saying to him. I fight against the urge to open the door and defend Maverick. Nothing Maverick could've done *warrants him talking to him that way, but I don't. I know firing back at him would likely only make things worse on Mav and that's the last thing I want for him.*

What kind of parent yelled at their kid like that? Hell, I understand not liking decisions they make or their behavior, but how could you not like your own flesh and blood?

Maverick's body slips into the backseat next to me, the look of apology in his eyes as he looks over at Dean murmuring an apology.

I can sense my mother's sadness watching the exchange, feeling terrible for how he was treated. She reassures him it's okay and that she's glad to have him joining us as she backs out of the driveway.

As much as my mom doesn't like the decisions I make, she's never once talked to me the way Maverick's father did just now.

I want Maverick to know he doesn't need to feel embarrassed or alone. In a bold move, I reach over and fold my hand over his resting in his lap. I can see his body tense out of the corner of my eye as he glances toward Dean. Finding us alone, he turns his head to look at me. I don't want to see the rejection on his face, so I keep my eyes trained out the window.

I'm not sure what I expected him to do after that but when I feel his hand turn over beneath mine, lacing our fingers together, I know it isn't that. The butterflies in my stomach take off. I tell myself repeatedly this doesn't mean to Maverick what it means to me. He is only holding onto the closeness I am offering him, something he obviously hasn't felt in a long time.

What he doesn't know is what he is giving to me in return. Hope. Hope that he will someday see me as more than Dean's sister, how much I care about him, and that he will eventually let me in.

Hope that someday he will feel for me the same way I feel about him.

Thinking back to that memory, my eyes run up Maverick's stomach, to the subtle rise and fall of his chest up to his face. His eyes are closed, and his long dark eyelashes are feathered out along his cheek. I know by the quietness of his breath, he's asleep.

He looks peaceful, and in that moment, I'm grateful I can keep the monsters lurking around the corners at bay.

At least for tonight.

Chapter Four

MAVERICK
Three Years Ago

Sweat drips from my brow and down my back as the sunshine beats down on me. Music blares from my headphones as I feel the wheels of my skateboard click over the cement beneath me.

I wipe the sweat dotting my forehead on the sleeve of my T-shirt. It's my first week living in Everton. My first week living in our new house, going to a new school, and here I am hanging out with my new friends.

Or I should say I'm trying to.

To be honest, I have no interest in making friends. Fuck, I don't even want to talk to people most days. I'm just sick of being inside, fed up *with listening to my dad do nothing but bitch at me. When the kid from my Biology class offered for me to hit up the skate park with him and a couple of friends, I jumped on the chance to get out of the house.*

I told him I'd meet them there. I didn't even care that it's eighty-two degrees outside. There are three weeks left in the school year and I know if there's any chance of me having a decent summer, I want to take him up on the offer knowing this friendship would likely get me out of the house more this summer.

"Mav, hey! What's up, man?" I hear Dean's boastful voice over the music as I remove my earbud, skating toward where he's standing.

There are people milling around downtown, walking along the boardwalk near the river. I maneuver my board around a couple walking, approaching me.

"Woah, asshole. Watch where you're fucking going." I hear shouted from behind me.

I quickly swerve, not wanting to crash into the person next to me. Bailing on my board, I lean back and come to a stop as a sea of brown hair and tan skin flies past me. The black Volcom hat covers her head as she turns back toward me grinning.

"What the hell?" I mutter.

"Ryan, why don't you go somewhere else? Like, I don't know, the mall?" I hear Dean shout. My brows furrow as I glance over at him, realizing he's chastising her.

Kicking the heel of my board, I grab it and walk toward where Dean and a group of guys are standing.

"You know her?"

"That's my sister and the biggest pain in my ass."

"Do I look like the type of girl who wants to spend her Saturday shopping? Get fucking real."

As if I wasn't distracted enough by the sheen of sweat covering her tan skin, her smart mouth and unfiltered thoughts would do it for me. My eyes follow her, watching as her hair blows in the wind behind her.

She must be able to sense my eyes on her, watching her, as she skates around the people walking along beside her. Glancing over her shoulder, her eyes fall on mine as a small smile curls around the edge of her lips. It's like she just punched me in the gut.

"Dude, eyes off. That's my sister. Don't be getting any ideas because it ain't gonna fucking happen. Not with me around."

Breaking eye contact, I come face-to-face with a stern Dean. He must be beating teenage boys off with a stick because one look at her, you'd have to be blind not to be captivated by her beauty.

Within five seconds of being near Ryan, I know she's dangerous for me. It's like playing with fire and God help me, I like the idea of getting burned.

Waking up the next morning, my body feels still from sleeping with my arm stretched beside me. My shoulder feels like there's a giant knot in it and I just want to get up and stretch.

As soon as I move, I realize the error of my ways. My eyes jolt open and come face-to-face with a sleepy-eyed Ryan. My mind races through all the events that occurred last night and how I ended up asleep in her bed.

Even with my discomfort from my sleeping position, I can't remember the last time I slept so well. The side of her mouth curves up in a small smile as my lip curls up mirroring hers.

"Morning," I whisper. "I'm sorry. I remember us talking one minute and before I know it, I'm passed out in your bed."

Rolling onto my side, I lean in close to where Ryan is lying and do my best to climb over her. As soon as my leg is positioned on the other side of her body, I press my mouth against her ear.

"I never thought I'd end up half naked and in your bed, Ryan Blake. Maybe in my dreams, but never in real life."

I can hear her suck in a deep breath, as I plant my foot on the floor next to her. Careful to avoid flashing her an embarrassing image of me, shirtless, sporting my massive boner, I adjust my cock so it's pressed against the waistband of my shorts and turn to face her.

"I guess I should probably head back over to your brother's room. Neither of us need an angry Dean on our hands."

She doesn't say anything, so I find myself scanning her face for any clue as to what she might be thinking. Her skin is soft as her eyes blink lazily from her tiredness. I want so badly to crawl back into bed next to her. It's not even from wanting to be with her sexually. Even though I could feel a spark of something more between us when I touched her. Lying next to her, falling asleep with her by my side, was the first night I've felt a sense of calmness since before my mom passed away.

I don't want to lose it, which makes walking back into Dean's room much more difficult.

Slipping out of her bedroom, I'm careful when I close the door and enter Dean's room. He's still asleep and the sound of me entering his room doesn't faze him in the least.

Kneeling on the makeshift bed I had set up on the floor, I adjust the pillows and lie my head back. The hardness from the floor causes my back to ache, but I don't complain.

Reaching over, I slide my phone out of the pocket of my jeans. I'm surprised when I see it's after eight in the morning. I know Ryan and I ran the risk of being caught, but I didn't regret it.

I never would.

There is a missed text from a number I don't recognize. Opening it up and reading the message, I'm able to piece together who it's from. The weight of my impending decision making it even more difficult.

Last night I opened myself up to Ryan about what my life is like at home. Knowing I'm so close to graduating, I've been keeping my head down and focusing on each day bringing me one day closer to getting out of this hell hole. I'm eighteen now, which means there's nothing keeping him from kicking me out. The fact of the matter is, it's the only place I have to go.

Last week we had an army recruiter visit our high school talking to us about enlisting. I'd be lying if I said I hadn't considered it as an option. He said because of my grades, I would be eligible to graduate early and enlist right away.

After fights with my father like the one we had last night, there's nothing I want more than to get out of this town. Then, when I think about Ryan and after the night we spent together, it makes it harder to consider leaving. I've spent the past five years keeping my distance; I've stayed away but she's eighteen now.

I could run the risk of pushing away the only friend I have here, to fulfill the ache my heart has been craving.

Rolling over, I push on my hands and move to stand. Looking over at Dean, he has the pillow draped over his face and his arm slung across the bed. I opt to send him a text as I fold up the blankets on the floor and slip out of the door.

I pause, standing outside of Ryan's room. I think about what she looks like in there, sleeping in her tank top and boxers, sprawled out on her bed. I picture her with her hair fanned out around her as her chest softly rises and falls with each of her shallow breaths.

I fight against the urge to open the door and crawl back into bed next to her as I walk down the hallway and out the front door.

The sun has started to rise and the birds chirp as I grab my skateboard from against the side of the house. Opting to walk, I take in the scenery around me and inhale the crisp spring air as I prepare myself for what is waiting for me at home. After the argument with my father last night, I know I shouldn't waste any time doing the chores he has for me.

When I'm home, I make a dash for the kitchen I open the cabinets and fridge, quickly taking inventory and making a mental note of everything we need before grabbing the credit card left out for me on the counter.

Not bothering to stick around for long, I head back out the door and make the trip to the corner store a couple blocks up the street deciding it's best to get it done now before he wakes up angry.

Later that night after I met up with Dean and some of our friends to celebrate his birthday, we ended up checking out a concert in Des Moines. It's after eleven by the time I make it home and I'm thankful when I find my father already asleep.

My phone vibrates from where it's sitting on the nightstand next to my bed.

"What's up?"

"What are you doing? You sound like you're sleeping. Dude, it's Saturday night. Wake the hell up!" Graham voice booms through the phone.

"Nah, just got home a little bit ago. Where the hell are you?"

I can hear someone shout his name as he mutters, "hang on, baby." I can only assume he's talking to his girlfriend, Halle.

"You going to answer the question or sit there and smack your lips in my ear?"

"Sorry, man. She can't keep her hands off me." I roll my eyes.

"Anyway, I'm in Everton for the night. We're at a party over at my buddy's house. He says he knows you. Castle, you know him?"

"Yeah, I know him. We don't run together but I know who he is."

"Well, you should come up. Castle mentioned Nadia was coming out and you know Ryan will be with her."

Graham is one of my good friends. We met when Dean and I were at the dirt track near Arbor Creek last year. He doesn't live close to us, so we don't see him often, but when the weekend comes he always makes sure he invites us to whatever party he'll be at.

He's the only person who knows how I feel about Ryan. It's because he's too observant for his own damn good and nothing gets past him.

He would never say anything to Dean, only for the fact he would want me to be the one to do it. He'll spend his time annoying the shit out of me until I do.

"I was just about to put in a movie," I lie.

His throaty laugh filters through the phone. "You're a liar. I know you want to see her tonight so don't give me that shit."

I don't bother to say anything because he's right.

"Alright," I say, rolling over checking the time on the alarm clock next to me. It's a quarter 'til eleven. "I'll take my dad's truck and leave here in a few."

Knowing my dad is in bed now, he will never have any idea I'm leaving. There's about an hour left of her birthday and nothing will keep me from ending it the way she started it.

With me.

Chapter Five

RYAN

"Happy Birthday to you," Nadia sings.

My eyes narrow into slits as I glance over at her. I don't normally give a shit about birthdays but turning eighteen is a big day for me.

"Don't give me that look. You're fuckin' eighteen now. How excited are you about tonight?"

I feel like we've been waiting for today forever. Mostly because in exactly a week, I'll be sitting in that chair getting my first tattoo. I'm so pumped, I can hardly stand it.

"I'm excited, alright? You haven't even told me what the plan is, only how it's going to be the party of the year," I sigh, rolling my eyes before flashing her a smile.

"Chill, will ya?" she retorts, drumming her hands against the steering wheel as we pull up to a stop light. "Castle said we could have a party at his place. His parents are gone and you know it's far enough out of town, it's not likely it will get busted."

Damon Castle is in our grade and has spent the past year doing anything to try and impress Nadia. Unfortunately for him, she doesn't seem too interested in anything but keeping him firmly in the friend zone. He hasn't taken the hint though.

She slips her arm behind the seat and grabs a gift bag before shoving it at me.

"I thought we decided no gifts?"

"I can't believe you thought I wouldn't get you a birthday present. It's not a big deal."

Reaching into the bag, I wrap my hand around the neck of a bottle and pull it out.

"Are you serious?" I laugh, holding the bottle of whiskey in my hand.

"Happy fuckin' Birthday!" she cheers, slowing the car down to pull onto the gravel road leading to Castle's house. I'm not usually one to drink when we go to parties, but I tell myself tonight will be different. What will one or two drinks hurt?

Pulling up the narrow drive, she guides her car to park behind a black Camaro.

"Oh, yeah, I forgot to tell you, Maverick should be here before too long," she says nonchalantly.

Dropping the bottle into my lap, I glance over at her. She clearly finds the look of surprise on my face comical. Holding the bottle between my thighs, I unwrap the plastic around the top and unscrew the bottle. Wrapping my hand around the neck again, I take a swig. I force my eyes closed as the burn slides down my throat, warming my body instantly.

Lifting the bottle toward Nadia, I nod my head asking if she wants some.

Shaking her head, she replies, "I am not drinking tonight. I want to make sure we get back to my place."

"You know Castle would make sure you got home alright or even give you a place to crash, if you wanted one."

Tilting her head back against the headrest, she lets out a sigh before peering over at me out of the corner of her eye.

"No," she states matter-of-factly. "It's not going to happen. He's such a player and you know it."

It's true. He's one of those guys who is good looking and knows it. He's used to getting everything he wants either from his parents or from girls tripping over themselves to get a minute of his attention.

Nadia, however, seems to be completely oblivious to his good looks and bad boy charm. I think it's what he likes about her, the chase.

I know her well enough to know if she gives in to him, she's worried she'll be made to look like one of the many girls in a long line of girls waiting for him to look their way.

Taking another swig of the whiskey, I screw the cap back on the bottle and slide it back into the bag. I decide against drinking any more, already feeling the slight buzz from the alcohol entering my bloodstream.

Stepping out of the car, I slam the door shut as a car pulls up behind us. By the looks of the cars parked in the grass lining the driveway, we are a little late to the party.

Following Nadia up the narrow sidewalk wrapping around to the back patio, *Seether* blares through the speakers when we enter through the door. People are standing around the kitchen, laughing with red cups in hand. I spot a few people I recognize as "happy birthdays" ring out over the music. I hold up my middle finger to everyone, which earns me a few laughs in return.

I spot Castle pushing his way through the crowd of people playing beer pong on the island. His eyes brighten when he sees Nadia.

He clearly takes her off guard when he wraps his arms around her, tilting his head down toward her neck. I'm not sure what he said to her but a moment later, she pushes him away jokingly. I choke out a laugh as I see the smile on her face and the pink shades highlighting her cheeks. As much as she might try to act like she isn't interested, I can say her reaction to him says something else entirely.

A hand wraps around my waist, pulling me backward. I quickly spin around coming face-to-face with Maverick's sinful grin.

"Rebel."

My eyes narrow at him, trying to cover my smile as I glance over his shoulder to see who's with him.

"Graham invited me. As far as I know, he won't be here. When I left him earlier, he was heading home," he clarifies, picking up on my question. I hadn't planned on drinking but having Dean show up would be a fuckin' buzz kill.

Cheers ring out behind us as I peer over my shoulder to see Graham slam a cup of beer. Adjusting my hat, I turn back to face Mav.

He takes a step closer, leaving an inch between us. The heat of our bodies pressed in close radiates between us as he reaches out, holding his hand on my hip. He's so much taller than me so I tilt my head back to make eye contact with him as he leans in close to me.

"Did you have a good birthday?"

His breath feathers against the shell of my ear and I struggle to control my body's reaction to him. Wrapping my hands around his wrists, I struggle to keep hold of my composure.

"The best," I mouth to him. He winks at me, which makes my stomach flip flop.

The shift between our relationship is different after last night but I somehow feel closer to him.

I can feel eyes on us as I look over to where Nadia is standing. I'm not surprised when I find her staring at the two of us with a smile on her face.

"Will you come with me for a few minutes?" Maverick asks. My eyebrows furrow at his question. I was certain after last night we agreed keeping our friendship on the down low would avoid any ridiculous reactions from Dean. Let's be honest though, nothing stays quiet in a town the size of Everton.

"Yeah, sure."

I hold up my hand to Nadia, signaling to her I'll be right back. She's already chatting with our friends so knowing I'm sneaking away with Mav has her shooing me away.

Maverick leads me outside to the pickup truck parked off to the side of the driveway. It's cooler, the sun has long since gone down, and the crisp breeze hits me in the face.

Holding my hands up to my mouth, I use the heat from my breath to warm my skin.

"Climb in quick. I have something I want to give you and it should still be warm in here."

He grabs the door handle and waits as I climb inside, shutting the door behind me. My eyes follow him as he jogs around the front of the pickup and slides in on the bench seat next to me.

Turning the key in the ignition as the lights dim in the cab, my eyes connect with Maverick's in the darkness and I feel like my heart could beat out of my chest with just one look. He's always had the ability to take my breath away, feeling like the wind was knocked out of me.

"I was thinking we could go for a drive?"

His deep voice does crazy things to my body. Rubbing my lips together, my eyes travel down his jaw to his lips before glancing back up at his. I hope he's thinking the same thing I am, I want to kiss him so badly. I have ever since last night when he was in my room.

I can't form words, so I respond with a simple nod of my head.

He backs out of the driveway and takes the gravel road toward the edge of town. I recognize where we're going as soon as we get closer. It's been a while since I've been down here. Growing up, I would take my skateboard and skate along the river banks. Nadia wasn't big into skating, but she'd always come with me. Maverick and Dean would often be here, although I made it a point to stay away from my brother no matter how much I wanted to be near Mav.

"I didn't expect you to be here tonight," I say, cutting through the silence.

Veering off, he pulls into a small parking lot overlooking the river and puts the truck in park. It's dark, leaving only the moonlight casting a soft glow onto the water as the muted stars twinkle overhead.

He nods his head. "Graham told me about the party. I didn't want to miss the chance to give you this," he says, turning on the dome light and handing a box to me. It's wrapped in black and silver wrapping paper.

"You didn't have to get me anything."

"I know I didn't have to." He bites down on his lip as his eyes meet mine. "I wanted to."

Peeling back the paper, my eyes dart up to Maverick's as I run my tongue over my lower lip. My heart starts to stutter as I continue to pull the paper back revealing a pack of drawing pencils and a sketchbook.

My heart warms as I run my finger over the edge of the notebook. He knows how much my art means to me. I've always felt like the people around me didn't understand it. How do I find the words to thank him for a gift that is so perfect?

"I hoped you would draw something for me."

His words draw my attention away from the sketchbook to his eyes.

"Is this like on Titanic? Do you want me to draw you like one of my French boys?" Raising my eyebrow at him in hopes he catches my humor.

"You just want to see me without my shirt on again," he jokes.

My lip curves up at him beneath the muted light.

"What is it you want me to draw for you?"

"Anything. I want it to have meaning, and I know whatever you come up with will blow me away."

I can feel the heat spread up my neck at his compliment. My tongue skates across my lower lip wetting my skin.

"I don't know what to say. I mean, of course I'll draw for you. It's the least I could do to say thank you."

"You don't have to thank me."

"I think, if anything, I should be saying it to you. I've been thinking a lot after our talk last night. I have never opened up about the shit going on at home."

After all the years he has been friends with Dean, I can't believe that Dean doesn't know the full extent of what brought him here to Everton or what he's been living through at home.

He doesn't deserve the bullshit he's been handed and I'm grateful he trusted me enough to open up.

"I'm surprised you're even here. Won't your dad be mad at you for driving his truck?"

"I don't really care." His voice holds no emotion as he cuts straight to the point.

"As soon as Graham told me you'd be here, I wanted to be here, too. I knew after your conversation with your mom last night you were going out with Nadia. I wanted to be able to give you the gift, but I didn't know how or when I'd see you."

"You came because Graham told you I'd be here?" I ask, surprised. I don't even know if I fully listened to anything he said after that, my mind latching onto those words and holding onto them with all the strength I have in me.

"Yeah." His hand wrapped around the bottom of the steering wheel clenches tightly.

Reaching over, I wrap my hand around his and pull it so it's sitting between us. He never moves to let go and it reminds me of that day in the backseat of my mom's station wagon. His thumb traces circles on the side of my hand and I get lost in the way his rough fingertips feel against my soft skin.

I want so badly to slide across the seat and wrap my hand around his neck, pulling him closer to me. I picture the way his commanding lips would feel on mine, how perfectly our tongues would twine together.

The images in my mind detailing the scene so vividly causes my chest to heave as my heart rate picks up.

"What are you thinking about, Ryan?"

His words are harsh, demanding.

"I'm thinking about how fucking bad I want you to kiss me."

<h1 style="text-align:center">Chapter Six</h1>

MAVERICK

My lips stretch across my face at her honesty. She's never been one to shy away from saying what she's thinking or feeling.

"I've been dying to fucking kiss you for so long," I mutter, wanting to see her reaction when I give it back to her just the same.

This time though, I don't stop there.

"Get over here, Rebel."

There is a moment of hesitation as her eyes dart to mine. Her tongue darts out, skating across her lower lip as she glances down at mine.

"Now."

Her eyes brighten, and I can see her smart-ass remarks forming in her head. I fully expect for her to argue with me on this, to fight me in some way not liking how I'm ordering her around.

No, the words do the exact opposite, spurring her into action. She quickly sets her gift on the dash before turning to kneel on the bench seat crawling closer to me. She takes me by surprise though when she swings her leg over mine, climbing above me.

I should've known if I gave her an inch she'd take a mile.

"Now what?"

Growling, I wrap my hand in her hair and pull her closer until her lips are a breath away from mine. The proximity and our now heavy pants cause the windows to fog up, which is fine. Anything to keep the world outside the truck away from us.

I'm only focused on the look of desire on Ryan's face and the way she's biting her lower lip in anticipation. Her eyes flutter back and forth between my eyes and my mouth, waiting for the moment when I'll finally put us both out of our misery.

Skating my palms down her sides, my fingers dig into her hips as I drag her closer to me. Her heat pressed against my growing length. I can feel every struggled breath as her chest rises and falls against mine.

As much as I would love to take her right here, I force myself to remember this isn't the place I want our first time to be. I reach up to wrap my fingers around the silky-smooth strands of her hair as I bring her lips to mine. Her hands fold around my neck as her legs tighten against my hips.

Running my tongue along her lower lip, she opens her mouth. I fight the urge to groan with how much I want her. Clenching my fingers into her hips, I hold her body closer to mine. Her fingers skate up my neck and into my hair, scratching along my scalp as a shiver rolls through me.

She pulls back momentarily, and I can see her run her tongue over her swollen lips. They're glistening wet and seeing them like that only turns me on more.

"Mav, I want you. I've only ever wanted you."

My eyes look around us, for the first time checking to see if we're still alone. It's dark and thankfully the tint on the windows make it difficult for anyone on the outside to see in. Pulling her against me, I move so she's lying down on the bench of the pickup truck.

The move takes her by surprise, but her arms pull me with her.

She lets go once she realizes I'm not going anywhere and moves to toss her hat somewhere on the floor, not caring or paying much attention.

"Last chance."

Maybe I'm paranoid but I know when we cross this line, there will be no going back. We won't be able to safely go back into whatever we are at this moment or even before last night.

Truth be told, I'm too far gone now. There's a peace that has come from being near Ryan. The fire inside her lit something in me that has been cold and dark for a long time.

Grabbing hold of the front of my shirt, she wraps her fist in the cotton material and pulls me close to her. I take in the glint in her eyes from the lights on the dashboard as they run over my face.

Her leg hitches around my hip, pulling me closer between the apex of her thigh. The move brings us so close there's not even a sliver separating us. I know she can feel how turned on I am as her eyelids lower with desire.

"You shouldn't have done that, Rebel," I whisper before opening my mouth to trace my tongue along her chest. She keeps my head pressed against her as I make my way up her neck.

"You taste as good as I expected. Like heaven and hell and everything I shouldn't want but I do."

I know after one taste of her, there's not a snowballs chance in hell I'm going to be able to forget her. I won't ever be able to recover.

I've thought about what it would be like to have Ryan for one night for a long time. Since moving to Everton, I've found myself searching for a way out of the darkness I've felt. After losing my mom, it left a hollow feeling in my chest where my heart was. I find myself craving the way she makes my heart beat out of control, a reminder that I'm still alive.

Pushing the material of her shirt up, I lean forward and run my tongue over her breast peeking out the top of her bra. Pulling the cup down, I run my tongue softly around her pert nipple. She smells just as good as she tastes and I'm acting out of impulse now, wanting more of her. I alternate between sucking and flicking my tongue, taking my time to learn what she likes.

"Holy shit," she mutters as her body trembles. Her fingers lace into my hair, holding me closer to her.

Kissing a line across her chest, I give her other breast the same attention as she grinds against me. My cock is begging for attention, making it difficult to focus on anything but how good it would feel to take her right here.

Her hands sneak down to the button of her jeans. Popping the first button and unzipping the zipper, she slides the denim over her hips.

I can spot the lace of her underwear and the thought has my body aching to have more of her.

Dragging my knuckle along where the lace covers her pussy, I feel the wetness seeping through the material. Sucking in a quick breath, I bite my lip to cover my moan before my finger disappears inside her.

"Damn," I murmur, once my finger is buried to the hilt.

She squirms in the seat as her cries become desperate for me to continue. Her eyes squeeze shut as she reaches her hand out for me, looking for something to hold onto.

My hand pumps into her as her moans pick up, filling the small space. The heat between us in the small space causes sweat to trickle down my forehead.

I keep my focus on her, to all the ways her body reacts to my touch, to the trembles of her stomach as she clenches around me.

"Ryan," I croak.

The battle I've been fighting with myself to take her right here is starting to win out.

Holding onto the edge of the seat, I tilt my head close to her ear and whisper, "It's taking everything in me not to say fuck it and take you right here. You deserve better though. I promise the first time we're together, it will be everything you deserve for it to be."

Her hands hold both sides of my face as she looks me deep in the eyes. Warmth grips my chest, feeling the strength of her emotions shining back at me. I didn't just tell her she was worthy of more; I told her I was prepared to give it to her.

I press a kiss against her lips. This one is filled with more force and passion than our last. Changing the angle of my hand, I rub circles over her clit and feel her heat tighten around me. Her body trembles with her release as her tongue plunges into my mouth, tangling with mine. My heart stammers in my chest as I hold her close to me.

The sound of Ryan's phone ringing jolts me out of the moment, feeling like a bucket of ice over my head. Ryan's hand wraps around my neck, pulling me closer to her.

"It's okay, just ignore it."

Her breath comes out in harsh pants and for a second, I consider doing as she says. I want more than anything to forget the world outside this truck and be here with her.

As soon as the phone stops ringing, a quiet ding follows, signaling a text message just before the ringing starts again.

"You sure you shouldn't get that?"

She reaches over, picking up her phone from where she tossed it on the floor and swipes the screen as she answers with a frustrated hello.

Ryan's eyes fly to mine, and I know with just one look that what we started tonight has ended. With her hand pressed against my chest, she mouths "we need to go" and I can feel my heart drop to the pit of my stomach.

I try not to read into the trepidation in her voice as she asks Nadia what's wrong, but when I hear Nadia shout Dean's name I'm reminded why this was a dangerous path for us to go down.

Now my only fear is if I were to lose them both.

Chapter Seven

RYAN

Pulling up into the driveway a few minutes later, I spot Dean and Nadia standing together. Nadia's hand flies around, pointing her finger at him. She's clearly upset and for a minute, I want to appreciate her having my back in whatever their heated exchange is about.

Adjusting my shirt, I open the door to Mav's pickup and slide out of the passenger seat.

"Ryan, what the hell are you doing?" Dean steps out from the other side of the truck. The lights lining the driveway are enough for me to see the slight tic in his jaw. I'm not sure how to answer the question so I opt to go with the safer route.

"What do you mean? Nadia is throwing me a party for my birthday. We just made a quick trip to the store to get some juice for our drinks." I decide to play it off like it's no big deal.

His eyes bounce back and forth between Maverick, standing at the front of the truck, to me. I can feel my skin heat as I struggle to remain cool. I know if he senses something is off, he'll lose it.

"When did you get here, man?" Maverick asks, sounding a lot more calm and collective than I do.

"A few minutes ago. Ryan, Mom knows you aren't at Nadia's. You need to get home. Now." He punctuates the end, his jaw set as his eyes narrow at me. I can tell whatever is waiting for me at home won't be good.

I purposely blocked my parents' calls, sending them all to voicemail. It was a risky move, but I figured if they found out I wasn't really at Nadia's, I wanted to make it worth it. I didn't expect for them to send Dean after me though.

"When were you going to tell me you've been seeing my sister behind my back?"

Dean's normally a jokester. He doesn't get angry, but I know he can be very protective of the people and things he cares about. I knew when he found out about my feelings for Maverick, he would not be happy.

"What are you talking about?"

"Do you think I'm fucking stupid, dude? Don't stand here and insult me," he spits, approaching Maverick, pushing him against the chest, caging him in against the front of the truck.

Maverick lets out a deep breath before glancing over at me. I can see the apology on his face knowing there's no way he's going to lie to Dean. He knows something is up and I agree lying to him would make it worse.

"It's not what you think," he says.

"Excuse me," Dean spits. "You better clear it up real fucking quick, dude. If I find out you're using her as another piece of ass, I'll knock your fucking head off."

I watch as Dean takes a step closer, bumping his chest against Maverick's, leaving only a breath between the two of them. Dean is challenging him and Maverick isn't backing down, even though I know he doesn't want it to lead to a fight.

"Dude, do you honestly think I'd treat Ryan like that, of all people?" I can hear the note of sincerity in his voice and I hope I'm not reading into it. Maverick holds his hands up, pressing them against Dean as he pushes him back, trying to reason with him.

"You're damn right it's not like that. You better stay the fuck away from her. Do you hear me? She doesn't need you dragging her into your hell."

"Dean, knock it off. You don't know what the hell you're talking about. Even if I was seeing Maverick, it's none of your fucking business. Chill out!"

It's as if my words fall on deaf ears as they stand nose-to-nose. Seeing them like this forces my feet to move, as I push my way in between the two of them and use my arms to separate them.

Maverick's eyes are bright with fury, but I know he would never do anything to hurt Dean. He's more hurt at the words he's used.

"She's better than you and we both know it. Stay the fuck away from her or I'll see to it that it doesn't happen myself."

My head snaps over to Dean, pissed he would try to intervene even if we went around him and his commands.

"Like hell you will. Shut the fuck up, Dean."

I know Maverick hadn't opened up about his life, but Dean is onto him. I can see the pain on Maverick's face at the mention of the shit he has going on at home.

Dean turns, facing me. "You better get your shit now and get home before Mom finds out what you were really up to tonight."

I never take my eyes off Maverick. His eyes are focused on the ground. His expression is hard as stone, not letting a single emotion give away what he's feeling. I want to knock Dean on his ass for talking to Maverick like that and wrap my arms around him, hating the direction our night has gone.

This is all my fault.

Stepping around Maverick, I open the door to the pickup. Reaching in, I grab my hat and cell phone from where it's lying on the floor. Pulling the snapback on my head, I click the button on the side of the phone to find thirteen missed calls from home.

Dean wasn't lying when he said our parents knew I wasn't at Nadia's tonight. I turn to Maverick.

"Will you text me?" I whisper.

He doesn't say anything and I'm silently begging him to respond. To say something that would show Dean this is not what he thinks. Even though he doesn't like the two of us together, that Maverick would never hurt me, and this means more to both of us. Maverick not doing anything only proves the point Dean's trying to make.

That no matter what Maverick may want, he's no good for me.

I look over to Nadia and the look on her face mirrors everything I'm feeling inside. Her heart is breaking for me knowing how one second, I was on cloud nine and then the next, it was like a hail storm, where everything has come beating down around me.

Nadia and I walk down the driveway as I round the front of her car, opening the passenger door.

"I'm sorry," she mutters, running her hand through her hair.

"Don't be," I interrupt, knowing she is somehow finding a way to blame this on herself. "I guess it's best he found out now before things went too far."

Pulling the car door closed behind me, I reach over and click the seat belt into place.

I can feel the lies on the tip of my tongue. Things had gone too far tonight. We had stepped over a line together.

My chest aches as my stomach bottoms out, knowing this may very well be the last time we are ever alone for a while, if ever. I know how important Dean is to Maverick and running the risk of losing him, I could feel his walls come back up and lock into place.

"What happened between you two tonight?" Nadia asks, turning the key in the ignition.

I didn't want to tell Nadia about it, at least not right now. I wanted to hold onto the little bits of my heart I still had, keeping them together, as it's being torn in two.

My eyes stay locked on Maverick. He's still standing with his back pressed against the pickup. His eyes are rooted to the ground, giving into the verbal lashing at the hands of my brother.

As if he can feel my eyes on him, his head turns toward me and lock on mine. I force myself to swallow what feels like a ball of cotton in the middle of my throat.

"Up until five minutes ago, it was the best night of my life. Now I don't know."

Chapter Eight

MAVERICK

With my arms crossed over my chest, I hear the rumble of Nadia's car starting and peer over to watch her pull out of the driveway. Despite the headlights shining brightly back at me, I can see Ryan's gaze at me from the front seat of the car.

I want so badly to walk away from where I stand next to Dean, listening as he yells, and pull her back in my arms. I hate that her birthday, this night together, has been ruined.

Dean continues to drone on about how he can't believe I went behind his back and deceived him. I want to argue with him, to point out all the ways his angry accusations are a load of shit, but I don't have it in me to even fight him anymore.

For the first time in all the years we've been friends, I feel as though every word he utters is betrayal.

My phone vibrates in my pocket. Slipping it out, I get a glimpse of the voicemail notification from my dad.

"I gotta go," I say, cutting him off in the middle of his tirade.

Dad had long since gone to bed when I left the house earlier. He never would let me take his truck, so the fact he's calling me not only says he is aware I'm not home, but he likely knows that I have the only possession he cares about anymore.

"We'll talk about this later," Dean says, spitting on the ground before adjusting his ball cap back around on his head.

I want to tell him there's nothing else to be said that he hasn't already got out, but I don't have the time or energy to stand here and argue with him. I don't even bother to see the look on his face. I cut across to the other side of the truck and climb inside. I fumble, trying to find the keys but find them still left in the ignition.

The light from the dash illuminates the small space and I notice right away what is left behind. Reaching over, I snag the sketchbook and pencils off the dash, setting them next to me.

The entire ride home I feel like I'm on edge. Gone is the high my body had been riding with Ryan in my arms. The euphoria of everything I had dreamt of is now being replaced with anxiety over what's to come when I get home.

As soon as I pull in the drive, I notice how the light on the front porch is on. The music plays on low, but I reach over and press the dial to turn it off. I'm the only one who can hear it, but somehow the fear creeps in.

The screen door flies open as I shift the truck into park. Standing in the doorway is my father. His greasy hair is swept to the side and there is a dark stain on the front of his white T-shirt. He runs his hand across his chest as he leans against the side of the door.

"Get the fuck in here!" he shouts. Shoving my hands in my pockets, I keep my head down as I walk toward the front of the house.

"When the hell did I give you permission to take my truck?"

I can tell he's been drinking from the way his words slur together.

"I'm sorry. I should've asked you before I took it. I didn't think it would be a big deal."

"A big deal," he grunts. "Even if you asked me, the answer wouldn't be any different than it is now. It's not yours to take, you ungrateful piece of shit."

I don't bother responding as I pass by him into the front door, knowing it's only going to make him more upset.

Walking through the kitchen, I drop the keys on the counter before heading down the hall toward my bedroom.

"Where the hell do you think you're goin', boy?"

I stop in my tracks and turn, not bothering to look up at him. Maybe there's a part of me avoiding the look on his face. Any resemblance of the father I knew growing up died along with my mom three ago.

"I asked you a question!" he roars.

Glancing up at him, I look him straight in the eyes and reply, "I am going to bed, if that's okay with you."

Raising my eyebrow, I wait for any sign he's going to argue with me on this. He grits his teeth, my response causing his jaw to tick. He takes the two steps, separating us, flattening his hand over my chest, pushing me against the wall.

His breath smells like liquor and I force a breath through my mouth to hide my disgust.

"You're a fucking ingrate, you know that? Get the fuck out of my house!" he hollers. "Get the fuck out of here and don't you ever bother coming back."

My nostrils flare as I bite back the urge to tell him to go to hell.

"If you come back here, I'll put you six feet under next to your mother."

And, that does it. There's no turning back now.

My hand curls into a fist and comes crashing against the side of his jaw. It happens so quickly, he doesn't even see it coming. The force behind the punch sends him falling back, crashing against the wall.

The alcohol flowing through his bloodstream is working as a disadvantage as he struggles to regain his footing. Pushing himself up right, he comes barreling back at me. He holds his arm against my chest, threatening to cut off my airway.

"She'd be disgusted by you. Look at you. There's not a day that goes by where I don't wish it would've been you instead of her. I hope you live out the rest of your miserable fucking life knowing it, too."

Shoving him back, I land another hard punch, this time right in the nose. The blood gushes, streaming down his face into his mouth. My chest heaves with every struggled breath as I work to regain my composure.

"If you ever talk like that about my mom again, I'll be the one to put you six feet under," I snarl.

Pain radiates through my fist as I struggle to open and flex it again. For a second, I consider the fact I likely broke my hand. By the looks of it, it's certainly banged up, but I think I may have gotten off easy.

He slumps to the floor, as I step over his haggard body collapsed against the wall. I hurry to my room and quickly shove anything I care to take with me into my backpack. Slinging the bag over my shoulder, I grab my guitar from where it sits at the foot of my bed.

I'm surprised when I walk out of my room to find he's no longer in the hallway. The door to the bathroom is shut so I rush down the hall and out the front door. In my haste to get inside, I forgot to lock the truck.

Grabbing the sketchbook and pencils from where I left them on the bench seat, I shove them in my backpack with the rest of my stuff. I'm not sure what my next move is but I find myself walking toward Ryan's house, wanting to see her.

I'm running a risk going to her house, especially knowing her parents were up waiting on her, but I don't care though. I need to see her, I need to be closer to her. If I'm going to leave tonight, I want her to know how much she means to me.

I'm surprised when I turn the corner onto her block and I see her light on and Dean's off. I don't see his broken down pickup truck parked in the drive, so I can only assume he decided to stay out with Graham for a while.

Pulling out my phone, I shoot off a text to Ryan letting her know I'm here. A few minutes later, I see her figure fill the window, as she pulls the string drawing her blinds. She's dressed in a black tank top and a pair of red boxer shorts. She points with her finger toward the front door. Adjusting the guitar in my hand, I nod my head and walk up the steps. The locks click as she slowly opens the door, careful not to make any noise.

"Can I stay here?"

She nods but doesn't say anything more as she turns and leads me down the hallway. The floor creaks beneath our footsteps. Following her into her room, she turns off the light leaving only her bedside lamp on. I set my guitar and backpack near her closet and immediately move to pull her into my arms. Her body feels tense, but she melts into me easily.

I trail feather light kisses along her shoulder, over her cheek, and to her mouth. Tangling my fingers into her hair, I press my lips against hers. Her hand wraps around the front of my shirt, holding me close to her.

My tongue runs along her soft lips as she opens to me. She lets out a small moan before I break the kiss, keeping our foreheads pressed in close to each other.

"How are you?"

Her eyes peer up at mine, looking warm and happy. "I'm okay. Grounded for a week, but it could be worse. Is everything okay?"

Looking from me to where my bag sits on the floor and back up to me.

"It is now."

I can sense her hesitation to believe me. I trail my thumb along her cheek. She presses her face into my hand as she gazes up at me.

As much as I love the passionate and opinionated side of Ryan, I think I love this side of her even more. The soft side where she lets me in.

Running my thumb along her lip, I wince at the pain that shoots up my forearm. Ryan doesn't miss the move even though I quickly try to smooth it over.

"What the hell happened?" she asks, holding my hand out in front of her. Her slender fingers brush over the bruised flesh as her eyes bore into mine.

"Let's just say things didn't go over well when I got home."

"Maverick," she scowls, knowing exactly where this is going. "What'd you do?"

"He said some things he shouldn't have. Things about my mother. It's a mistake he won't make again."

"Why do I feel like what you're about to tell me is going to change everything?"

Holding my hand up to her mouth, she presses a kiss against my damaged flesh. Tingles spread up my arm and I find my breath caught in my throat.

"Ryan," I croak.

I hate what I am going to tell her next. I have no other options now. As much as I hate to do this, I know I don't have any choice.

"This isn't the first time my dad and I have gotten into it. It's just the first time it's escalated this far. Our last fight happened the night before we had career day at school," I say, looking up at her, pausing to take in the look on her face. "I spent some time talking to the army recruiter. I hadn't given much thought in what I would do after graduation, but we're just a few months away now. I have enough credits that I could graduate early, if I wanted to."

Tears fill her eyes knowing the direction this conversation is taking. I hate seeing her in pain.

"I'm going to go up north to Minnesota and stay with my aunt for a little while before I head out for basic training."

She lets out a deep exhale as she rubs her hands together before moving around me crossing the bedroom toward her door.

She raises her arm up, running her hand along her neck, rubbing the tension there before reaching out to lock the bedroom door. When she turns around, her eyes trail up my legs to my face. I can see it on her face, the desire, but I wait for what she's about to say.

"Will you stay with me tonight?"

Chapter Nine

RYAN

My heart feels like it's hammering out of my chest. After the way things got heated earlier tonight, I knew Maverick wanted my first time to be special.

Somehow, in a matter of just a couple hours, things have changed. After tonight, I don't know when I'll see him again and my heart aches even considering how long it will be.

His eyes are searching mine, looking for any hint that I may be second guessing this or hesitating. There isn't a single inch of my body that doesn't want him.

My parents are two doors down the hall and I know we're running a huge risk of getting caught, especially if Dean comes home. I don't care though because if this is all I have with him, I want him to leave me with something worth remembering.

I want to send him off with a piece of me no one else will ever have.

"Ryan," he whispers. The uncertainty in his voice crushes me, but I push it aside.

Closing the space between the two of us, his arms encircle my waist, holding me against him. His hands run underneath the hem of my shirt. My body trembles with the force of the shivers running through me.

My reaction to his touch is undeniable. Reaching down, I pull my tank top up and over my head. Maverick leans back, his eyes traveling from my stomach up to my chest and back down again.

His hands loosen around my waist and his fist covers his mouth. He tries to hide the muffled groan. I love seeing his reaction; the desire in his eyes, the warmth of his skin to the way he subtly bites his lip.

I relish in it. I crave more of it.

Sliding my thumbs along the waistband of my boxers, I push the material over my hips until they fall to the floor, standing before him in nothing but my sports bra and lace underwear.

When Maverick sees me gathering the only scrap of material covering me up, he reaches forward and grabs my arm, pulling me quickly into him.

A smile breaks out across my face and a smirk graces his lips.

"You are trouble," he mutters, looking up at me and then back down to my mouth.

Leaning forward, I press a kiss against his mouth, swallowing his moan in the process. His hands roam over the curve of my ass; he squeezes the flesh in his hands pushing me closer against him.

"Are you sure this is what you want?" he asks when our mouths break apart.

"I'm sure," I say with every bit of confidence I have in me.

My eyes rake over his body, to the growing erection in his pants, as he kicks off his shoes and drops his pants near mine. I can't even control the desire pooling in my belly wanting to run my hand over him through his underwear.

When my eyes find Maverick's, his are bright with arousal as he pulls his shirt over his head. His abs flex and I can't hold back the urge to be near him any longer.

"We should lie on the floor. I don't want your parents to hear us, or worse Dean."

I push the thought of why Dean would be worse than my parents away because as much as I hate to hear it, he's right.

Grabbing blankets and a pillow from my bed, I lay them out on the floor. I can't even remember who moves first or maybe it's both of us, but it's as if we can't keep our hands off each other. Maverick's coarse hands running over my soft skin cause my body to shiver.

He helps me lie down on the floor next to him. Wrapping his hand in my hair, his mouth is back on mine, and I let my body soak up every ounce of his attention. I relish the feel of how his warm breath feathers over my mouth as our legs tangle together. He rubs his thigh between my legs, adding a friction which is making me go insane with how badly I want him.

His hand glides down my back, effortlessly unhooking my bra before his skilled hands take my breast in his. Everything he does to me has me going out of my mind wanting more.

"Maverick," I moan, before his mouth covers my pleas.

"Is this—" he pauses, hesitating. "Is this your first time?"

I nod as his hand disappears into my underwear as I grind against his palm. He mutters a quiet "fuck", feeling how ready I am for him before pulling his hand back. He quickly sheds his boxers and I follow along right beside him. I watch as he pulls a condom out of his wallet and quickly tears the wrapper open.

I bite down on my lower lip to smother my groan, seeing how sexy he is with his hard cock in his hand, before his body covers mine. When the head runs over my aching center, I feel like my eyes are going to roll back into my head.

"Ryan, I need you here. I need you with me."

My eyes open behind the haze of desire as he pushes his way into me.

"This will hurt for just a second, but then, I promise it will feel better."

I find myself wanting to ask him how he knows, but I don't want to ruin the moment knowing this may be our only time together. My body begins to tremble with need as Maverick trails a kiss along my collarbone, whispering it'll be okay.

Letting out a shaky breath, I give him a small nod as he continues. His eyes never leave mine as he pushes his way in. With every inch, I feel the grip he has around my heart tighten.

I wrap my arms around his neck wanting him closer to me, needing to hold onto this moment, preserve it forever, and never let it go.

"I'm going to move now, baby."

Nodding my head again, I seek out his mouth, pressing a hard kiss against his lips. He pulls out slowly before rocking his way back inside of me. With every thrust, I find my body relaxing, passing the threshold of pain, and riding the high of pleasure.

A quiet moan slips out of Maverick's mouth and I quietly beg him for more. Maverick releases a shaky breath, leaning back and watching as he fills me over and over.

"Ryan," he moans, reaching up to grab my breast in his hand. Covering his hand with my own, I can feel my release building with every hurried thrust. Judging by the hard look on Maverick's face, he's not too far behind me.

Adjusting his angle, he runs my nipple between his thumb and forefinger. The sharp pain is followed by pleasure as I release a moan. He quickly moves his hand up to cover my mouth.

"You have to keep quiet, baby."

Lights flicker before my eyes as I squeeze them shut as my body quakes with my release. I'm thankful Maverick hasn't moved his hand as he covers my muffled moan. Maverick continues to thrust into me, riding out his release before collapsing on top of me.

My hands wrap around him, my fingers trailing lovingly along his heated skin.

We lie together for a few minutes before Maverick pulls out of me. Reaching down, Maverick pulls a blanket from the bed onto the floor and covers us up together. It's a risky move falling asleep without getting dressed, but I don't have it in me to care anymore.

Maverick's arm slides underneath the pillow before he pulls me in closer to him. With my back pressed against his front, he wraps his arm around my chest. I hold onto him, soaking up anything he is willing to give me.

I hate knowing, in a few hours, when we both wake up, this will all be over. So much has happened in the span of only a few days. I went from knowing Maverick as my brother's best friend and my high school crush, to feeling something more with him. Something deeper than I have ever felt before and it scares me.

What scares me the most is the fear that when I wake up, when he's gone and moved on with his life, that I'll be left with only the memories of what it felt like to be in his arms. I'm afraid of never knowing what it will be like to love again. Even more, I'm scared that I'll never be able to heal my torn heart because I know he'll be the only one who can.

My thoughts eventually calm and the sleep, that seemed to elude me for over an hour, comes. Maverick's quiet snores and his warm breath against my neck soothe me into a deep sleep. When my eyes open the next morning, the warmth I felt was replaced by a bone chilling cold from not having his body against mine.

With the blanket wrapped around my body, I hold the material to my chest sitting up in a panic as my heart drops into the pits of my stomach. Immediately I search for his bag sitting near the closet, hoping and praying for some indication he is still here.

There's no way he could've left without saying goodbye.

My eyes fill with tears when I realize how wrong I am. It's as if my heart cracked open in my chest. I fall back onto our makeshift bed, curling my legs against my chest and cry until I am certain there isn't a drop of tears left in me.

A little while later, after I convinced myself to get up, I go through the motions of taking a shower and getting dressed. Standing beneath the hot spray, I cry as I wash away all traces of last night from my body.

Walking back into my room, the first thing I notice is the sketchbook and pencils Maverick gave me sitting on my desk. I feel my heart sink further when I notice the words written on the page.

Ryan,

If you're reading this, I know it means you woke up and found me gone. I'm sorry, fuck, I'm so sorry. I hope you know how much I wanted to be there, to be able to say goodbye to you. I hope you don't feel like last night didn't mean everything to me, because it did. If I'm honest, it meant the world to me to fall asleep next to you again, to feel the peace only you have been able to bring me.

I wish I was strong enough to stay, to look at you when tears streamed down your face as we said goodbye. I just couldn't do it though. I wanted the last memory to be of the love you had in your eyes last night.

I promise I'll carry it with me while I'm gone.
Love,
Mav

Clutching the sketchbook against my chest, I feel another wave of tears flow down my cheeks. I don't know how it's possible for me to cry any more than I already have, but I do.

I slide a pencil out from the box sitting on my desk and open to a clean page in my sketchbook. When the lead touches the paper, everything I had been feeling flows out of me and into my drawing. Maverick had asked me to draw him something, knowing anything I drew would mean something.

My heart feels like it's been torn in two. In that moment, I make a promise to myself never to forget this feeling. I'll carry the tattered pieces of my heart with me, keeping Maverick with me from this day forward.

I just wanted to help heal him, but in the end, he broke me.

To be continued...

Thank you for reading **TORN**! I hope you love Maverick and Ryan as much as I do.

You can continue their emotional conclusion Tattered, Book 2 in the Tattered Heart Duet.

If you enjoyed Torn, I would appreciate your help in spreading the word, including telling a friend. Reviews help readers find books! Please leave a review on your favorite site.

You can sign up for my newsletter to learn more about my new releases. You can also join my Facebook group, Brooke O'Brien's Rebel Readers Group, for exclusive giveaways and sneak peeks of future books. To join, visit:

www.authorbrookeobrien.com/follow.

Now, turn the page for a sneak peek of Tattered...

Tattered

A TATTERED HEART DUET #2

USA TODAY BESTSELLING AUTHOR
BROOKE O'BRIEN

Prologue

Mav,

Waking up this morning to find you gone has been hard to accept. I keep looking over at where you slept next to me, hoping I'd wake up and this will have all been a dream. You may not have believed in what was between us, but I did. I know how I felt every time you looked at me and kissed me.

I don't know when I'll see you again or if you'll ever come back home to Everton. Reading your letter, I find myself wanting to hold onto the hope you'll find your way back to me. As long as I have hope, I'll wait for you. I'm going to keep believing in what I felt for you since we first met and hope someday you'll come home to me.

Love,

R

Chapter One

MAVERICK
Four Years Later

It's been years since I've got a full night's sleep. As the days have passed, sleep is starting to feel like a distant memory. The nightmares that plagued me were just a reminder of the hell I was reliving when I was awake. After two tours, one in Iraq and the other in Afghanistan, these nightmares haven't seemed to let up. The only difference now is the monsters chasing me wear a new face.

Life has delivered a bitter pill that I haven't been able to swallow. It's hardened my heart, which when you're in the military, is exactly what you need to serve. If you let shit get you down or get lost in your emotions, you'll end up taking your eyes off the purpose of why you're here.

I know what can happen if you do. You make mistakes, and if you're not careful, you may end up being called home, and I'm not talking in the way you want to be either.

The heat from the humid air is stifling as sweat drips down my forehead. Crossing my arms beneath my head, I adjust the pillow as I close my eyes and enjoy a few minutes of silence.

My platoon and I are about seven months into our time in Kabul, Afghanistan. We're still waiting to hear the official word, but sometime in the next two weeks we should be making our trip back home and fuck if I'm not ready to set foot back on American soil.

"Night, wake up. You got a call."

The loud command bounces off the walls of the tent as I peek my eye open.

James peers his head into the tent. There's a look of surprise on his face as he nods his head toward the tent on the other side of our bunk.

Letters sent to me are few and far between, much less a phone call, so I know, like me, he's wondering what's going on. Once he sees I'm awake, his head disappears again. I wonder who the hell could be trying to get in touch with me.

Stepping out of the tent, my eyes glance at the picnic tables set up outside on the base. Several of the guys are sitting around, playing cards and shootin' the shit. There's not much to pass the time, but you'd be surprised at what you can come up with to keep your mind off what's going on outside the base.

My eyes connect with James standing off to the side. His arms are crossed as he looks on at the other guys playing a game of cards.

"Who is it?"

"No name, but sounded important."

I nod my head. I don't have a good feeling about this and I'd like to get this over with.

Stepping into the Communications Center, I pick up the phone and press the line, connecting the call.

"This is Maverick Night," I state, swallowing down the ball in my throat.

"Mav." It's hard to hear through this phone but I can make out the voice.

"Dean?"

"Yeah, buddy. I'm sorry to call you like this. It took jumping through some hoops to get in touch but listen, your grandmother contacted me yesterday. She was looking for some help in trying to reach you. Got some news for you about your dad."

He pauses for a moment, and I want to tell him to spit it out already. After our fight, I didn't talk to him for several months. When I got back home from basic training, there was a letter from him waiting for me along with one from Ryan. I know Dean holds a lot of regret for the way shit went down. I needed him to know me enlisting wasn't his fault.

Every time I've called him to check in, I fight the urge to ask him what I really want to know. How is Ryan? Is she seeing anyone? Does she miss me as much as I fucking miss her?

"He passed away, man. They're saying his liver failed."

His words rattle around in my head as I replay them over and over.

He is gone.

The mother fucker is actually gone.

I should be surprised at the age of fifty-three, but I know he stopped taking care of himself long before we lost my mom. Her passing away just sped up the process. He started drinking heavier, which led to his anger. I doubt he's even been to the doctor since I left, so any signs or symptoms likely went missed.

"Shit," I mutter, not knowing what to say. "What are the plans then?"

Running my hand over my face, I clench my hand around my jaw as I think of everything that needs to be arranged. The only people my dad had was his brother, Richard, who I don't think he's talked to in over fifteen years and my grandmother. The last thing I want to do is put this on her.

"We're still working it out. I'll help her get everything taken care of, man. No worries, I'll be there. Just let me know what you need."

"I'll figure out how soon I can get out of here. I'll try to give you a call later this evening after I talk to my sergeant."

Dean fills me in on his plan to go with my grandmother to figure out the details. Disconnecting the call, I scrub my hands over my face. I don't even know how I feel hearing the news. There's a part of me that almost feels relieved to know I won't have to face him again.

I walk across the base toward the Command Center, ducking my head as I step inside.

"Sir, do you have a moment?"

I've served the last two tours with Sergeant Jackson. He's grown to be more of a father to me than my own father in a lot of ways. I hold an immense amount of respect for him.

"Of course," he says, setting the papers he was shuffling through down on the table. "Everything alright?"

"I just took a call patched over to me from my friend back home. He wanted to let me know my father passed away yesterday. I was hoping I could talk to you about taking a short leave to help get everything in order."

"I'm sorry to hear about your father," he says.

I want to tell him his sympathy is not necessary, that he doesn't deserve anyone's sadness. Saying that will bring on an onslaught of unwanted questions, so I simply respond with a nod.

"You do what you need to do. We're about to button up things here before we follow you back home, too. Don't bother joining us. We'll see you back home in the States soon."

"That won't be necessary, sir. It should only be a few, three maybe four days at the most, depending on when I get a flight back home. I'd like to come back and finish with the rest of the guys."

"I figured you would say that, but I'll have to decline. We should be heading back shortly after anyway, and it wouldn't serve a purpose to bring you back only to have you return home in a short time. Go home, take care of what you need to, and report to the base when you get everything in order."

I don't press it further.

"I'll see what I can do to arrange you a flight first thing in the morning. Let me know if there is anything I can do before you take off."

Clenching my jaw, I nod my head and lean forward to shake his hand.

As much as I want to help finish things off here, I'm relieved to know my time left in this sandy hell is coming to an end very soon. It isn't until I'm back in my bunk packing that it hits me; this will be the first time in four years I will be back in Everton.

My mind floats back to the phone call with Dean and my thoughts of Ryan. I think about how she looked our last night together, standing outside of her house in the pitch black. Her hair pulled over her shoulder and her boxer shorts rolled at the waist, showing her smooth tan skin on her legs. I hated walking away from her the next morning, I couldn't even work up the courage to say goodbye. I hated knowing I was leaving the only peace I had found since my dad moved us to Everton.

Pulling out the only picture I have of her from my wallet, I sit down on the edge of the mattress. Running my finger along the worn edges, my heart warms looking at her. The edge of her lip is curled, the smirk lining her mouth.

Fuck, I miss her.

The next day was long. I was taken to Germany where I was delivered to the U.S. Army base, then later, boarded a flight bringing me back to the States. When I arrived in Des Moines, I texted Graham to see if he could pick me up from the airport. We had exchanged a few text messages throughout the day, so I knew he had an important meeting about the security company he and Dean were opening.

Feeling tired after all the traveling, I opted to hail a cab and head to the hotel just a few minutes away. The exhaustion was starting to set in, and I was ready to take a much needed nap.

Stepping outside, I'm met with a wall of humidity. Unlike the dry heat I am used to, this heat is completely different. I can feel the perspiration dotting my forehead the moment I step outside. A cab pulls right in front of me, and I send up a silent prayer of thanks it was this easy for me to catch a lift.

Adjusting my duffel bag on my shoulder, I glance down at my phone vibrating in my hand when the door of the cab swings open, hitting me in the arm. The force knocks my cell phone out of my hand and sends it crashing to the ground. My eyes wince as I watch it slide along the hard concrete.

"You really should pay attention to where you're walking."

I could remember that snarky tone anywhere, reminding me of the first day we met. My head jolts in the direction it came from. I'm not able to see her face, but I can tell by the back of her head it's her. She still has the same long, dark hair covered up by her usual backward snapback. She's dressed in her T-shirt, tied at her waist, paired with cut-off denim shorts and Chucks.

My eyes follow her movement as she leans forward to pick up her suitcase, carrying it around to the back of the cab and tossing it into the trunk. I can't help but eat up every inch of her skin. I'm drawn to the ink covering her arm to the dreamcatcher covering her toned thigh.

She looks so much like the girl I remember, but she's different, too.

Leaning over, I grab the back passenger door and hold it open for her, waiting for her to close the trunk and see me. Judging by her comment, I don't know that she realized it was me. There's no way in hell I'm going to let her get away without sharing a cab with her.

When her hands reach up to close the trunk, our eyes connect. Hers widen in shock as her mouth drops open.

"Mav."

My name comes out more of a question, as if asking herself if it's really me. She may look different, but I know I don't look like the same kid she said goodbye to either. My hair is shaved close to my scalp. The tattoos covering my arm are, in a lot of ways, thanks to her. Her artwork growing up inspired a lot of the pieces that are now forever etched into my skin. Her eyes roam over my body, to the duffel bag slung over my shoulder.

Nodding my head, I reply, "Ryan. It's good to see you."

I hold the door open and wave my hand in front of me, encouraging her to climb inside. Her eyes furrow for a moment before she quickly looks up at me. I'm waiting for the inevitable remark to come because when has Ryan ever ignored the opportunity to provide her smart-ass commentary?

"You followin' me around again, Maverick?" Her lip curls up on the edge and I fight off the urge to kiss the smirk right off her sexy mouth.

"Don't tempt me, Rebel." The double meaning is clear. She knows I'd follow her and not do a damn thing to hide it. I also am not even trying to disguise the look of desire on my face.

Pulling her sunglasses from where they are hung on the front of her tank top, she slides them over her face.

"I figured we could share a ride. I'm feeling a little nostalgic after the last time we took a ride together."

"You think you'll be able to keep your hands to yourself this time around?"

I wish I could see her eyes, so I could read her expression. I'm not sure if she's baiting me or if that's what she really wants.

Tilting my head in close to her neck, I let my breath feather across her skin as I whisper, "When I get the chance to put my hands on you again, Rebel, I promise it will be because we both want it. You may even find yourself begging for it."

Do you want to read more of Mav and Ryan's story?

Grab your copy of Tattered at: www.authorbrookeobrien.com/tatteredheart duet

BOOKS BY BROOKE

A Rebels Havoc Series

Brix
Sins of a Rebel
Tysin
Trey
Madden

Men of Blaze

Personal Foul
Reckless Rebound (Cocky Hero Club)

Tattered Heart Duet

Torn
Tattered

A Heart's Compass Series

Where I Found You
Lost Before You
Until I Found You

Now That I Found You
Where You Belong

Standalones (In order of publication)

Wild Irish

Learn more and purchase your copy at:
www.authorbrookeobrien.com/booksby-
brooke

PLAYLIST

Check out Brooke's writing inspiration, along with some of Mav & Ryan's favorites.

Scars – Papa Roach
Your Guardian Angel – Red Jumpsuit Apparatus
Only One – Yellowcard
Addicted – Saving Abel
Broken – Seether
Without You – Hinder
Life After You – Daughtry
Here Without You – 3 Doors Down
The Reason – Hoobastank
Second Chance – Shinedown
Alone – I Prevail

Listen to the Playlist on Spotify at:

www.authorbrookeobrien.com/torn

ABOUT BROOKE

USA Today Bestselling author Brooke O'Brien writes steamy and swoon-worthy new adult romances. She's best known for her sports and rock star romances.

Brooke believes a love worth having is worth fighting for, and she brings this into her stories where her characters risk it all for love.

When she isn't writing or falling in love with a new book boyfriend, you can find her spending time with her family, cheering on her favorite sports teams, listening to ASMR, or binge-watching the latest true crime documentary. She loves rockin' a comfy hoodie with leggings and believes the best days include a good nap.

Brooke loves connecting with readers and hopes you'll join her on her social pages or reader group to stay in touch. To follow Brooke and join her newsletter, visit authorbrookeobrien. com/follow.

ACKNOWLEDGMENTS

I have so many people I want to thank for helping me on this amazing journey. I'm grateful beyond words for everyone who has been there for me, especially those who took a chance on me in the beginning.

Thank you to my amazing readers for picking up my books and taking a chance on my stories. To everyone who has left a review, sent me a message or a comment, THANK YOU! I can't even begin to tell you how happy it makes me when I hear from you. To all the bloggers who support me and help spread the word of my releases, you matter! I couldn't do this without you and your love for books.

My Boys - Everything I do in this life is for you. I could never find the words to describe how much I love you.

Asha (a.k.a. Smash) - We've been through a lot together over the past few months, but I'm so grateful to have you as my sister bestie. Thanks for always being there for me, through the thick and thin. Love you!

To my AMAZING beta readers Giovanna, Julia, Erin and Ana - Thank you for sparing your time and reading Maverick and Ryan's story in the rawest form. You are always so honest with your feedback.

I owe a big hug and a thank you to my editor, Rox LeBlanc, and my proofreader, Julie Deaton, for helping me polish off this story and making it the best it could be. I appreciate all of you for being patient with me on this one.

To Kate - Thank you so much for being there for me. We may not always talk everyday, but I hope you know how grateful I am to have you as my friend.

To Najla Qamber with Najla Qamber Designs - Thank you to you and your amazing team! You are so incredibly talented and always such a pleasure to work with. You put up with me and my numerous changes, but always end up blowing me away by bringing my vision to life.

COPYRIGHT

is not authorized, associated with or sponsored by the trademark owners.

For information on subsidiary rights, please contact Tattered Ink Publishing at www.authorbrookeobrien.com.

www.ingramcontent.com/pod-product-compliance
Lightning Source LLC
Chambersburg PA
CBHW070514200726
48293CB00007B/2521